31143012230844
J 966.9 Golkar, G
Golkar, Golriz,
Nigeria /

DISCARDED

Main

COUNTRY PROFILES

NIGERIA

BY GOLRIZ GOLKAR

BELLWETHER MEDIA • MINNEAPOLIS, MN

Blastoff! Discovery launches a new mission: reading to learn. Filled with facts and features, each book offers you an exciting new world to explore!

BLASTOFF! UNIVERSE

BLASTOFF! Beginners — GRADE K

BLASTOFF! READERS — GRADES 1-3

BLASTOFF! DISCOVERY — GRADE 4

This edition first published in 2021 by Bellwether Media, Inc.

No part of this publication may be reproduced in whole or in part without written permission of the publisher.
For information regarding permission, write to Bellwether Media, Inc.,
Attention: Permissions Department,
6012 Blue Circle Drive, Minnetonka, MN 55343.

Library of Congress Cataloging-in-Publication Data

Names: Golkar, Golriz, author.
Title: Nigeria / by Golriz Golkar.
Other titles: Blastoff! discovery. Country profiles.
Description: Minneapolis, MN : Bellwether Media, 2021. | Series:
    Blastoff! Discovery. Country profiles | Includes bibliographical
    references and index. | Audience: Grades 4-6 | Audience:
    Ages 7-13 | Summary: "Engaging images accompany information
    about Nigeria. The combination of high-interest subject matter and
    narrative text is intended for students in grades 3 through
    8"–Provided by publisher.
Identifiers: LCCN 2020002011 (print) | LCCN 2020002012 (ebook)
    | ISBN 9781644872543 (library binding) | ISBN
    9781681037172 (ebook)
Subjects: LCSH: Nigeria–Juvenile literature.
Classification: LCC DT515.22 .G65 2021 (print) | LCC DT515.22
    (ebook) | DDC 966.9–dc23
LC record available at https://lccn.loc.gov/2020002011
LC ebook record available at https://lccn.loc.gov/2020002012

Text copyright © 2021 by Bellwether Media, Inc. BLASTOFF!
DISCOVERY and associated logos are trademarks
and/or registered trademarks of Bellwether Media, Inc.

Editor: Christina Leaf   Designer: Brittany McIntosh

Printed in the United States of America, North Mankato, MN.

TABLE OF CONTENTS

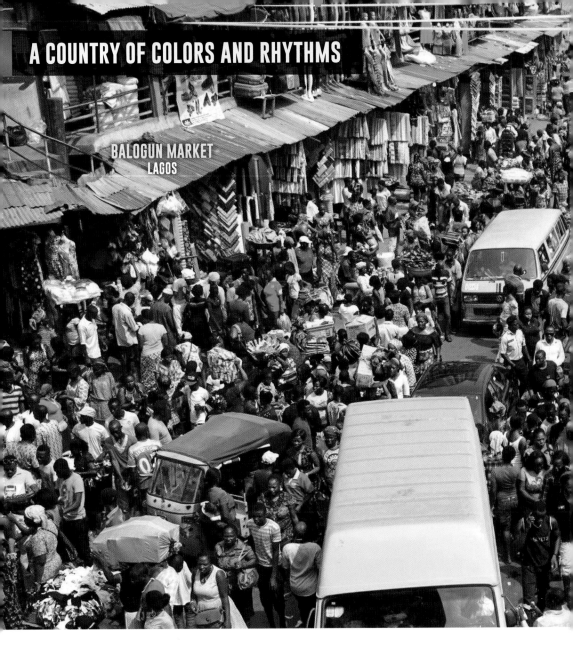

BALOGUN MARKET
LAGOS

A family wanders through the stalls of Balogun Market in Lagos, Nigeria. Colorful fabrics and handmade crafts are on display. After buying a few **souvenirs**, the family takes a break at a small *buka* nearby. The cozy local café serves them tasty *moi moi* bean cakes and tea.

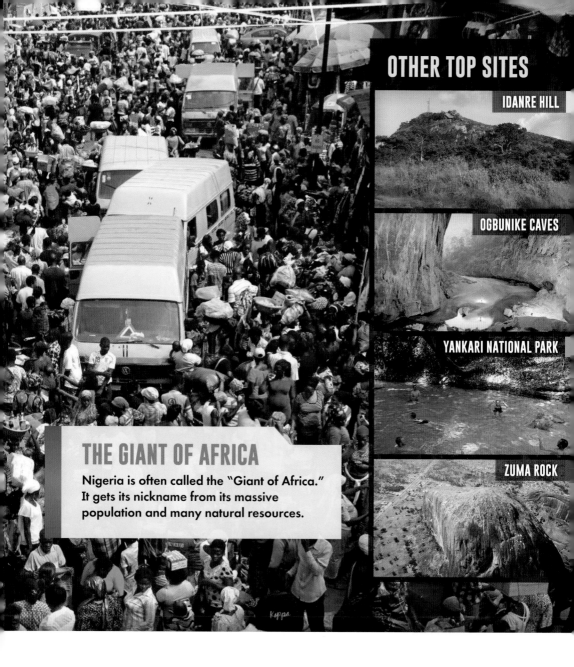

OTHER TOP SITES

IDANRE HILL

OGBUNIKE CAVES

YANKARI NATIONAL PARK

ZUMA ROCK

THE GIANT OF AFRICA

Nigeria is often called the "Giant of Africa."
It gets its nickname from its massive
population and many natural resources.

After their snack, the family heads downtown to Freedom
Park. They visit an art gallery inside the park. Then they relax
by the pond while enjoying the rhythmic drumming of live
reggae music. The colors, flavors, and music of Lagos are
a window to the lively country of Nigeria!

5

WHERE'S THE CAPITAL?

Lagos was once the capital of Nigeria. In 1991, the capital was moved to Abuja. A central location was chosen so that no single ethnic group would have too much power.

NIGER

KANO - - - ●

BENIN

NIGERIA

★ - - - ABUJA

IBADAN

LAGOS

GULF OF GUINEA

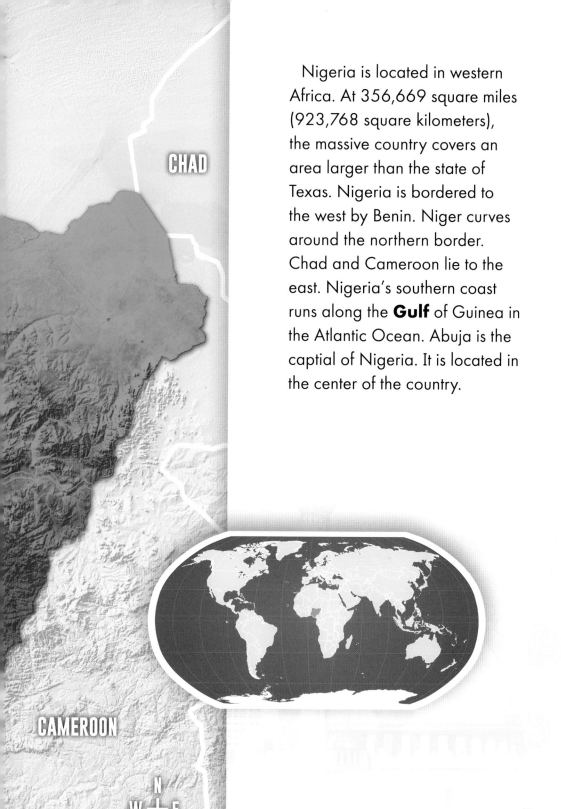

Nigeria is located in western Africa. At 356,669 square miles (923,768 square kilometers), the massive country covers an area larger than the state of Texas. Nigeria is bordered to the west by Benin. Niger curves around the northern border. Chad and Cameroon lie to the east. Nigeria's southern coast runs along the **Gulf** of Guinea in the Atlantic Ocean. Abuja is the captial of Nigeria. It is located in the center of the country.

CHAD

CAMEROON

N
W + E
S

LANDSCAPE AND CLIMATE

Nigeria is mostly covered with grassy **plains**. The Sokoto Plains span the northwest. The northeastern Borno Plains reach Lake Chad. Lowlands run along Nigeria's coast. Central Nigeria features hills and the Jos **Plateau**. The highest point,

= JOS PLATEAU

NIGER RIVER

CHAPPAL WADDI

N
W+E
S

Chappal Waddi, is found in the mountains along the Cameroon border. The Niger River winds through the country from the northwest. It drains into the Gulf of Guinea.

WHAT'S IN A NAME?

Nigeria is named after the Niger River, the third-longest river in Africa.

SANKWALA
MOUNTAINS

ABUJA
Average seasonal highs and lows

JANUARY
HIGH: 91 °F (33 °C)
LOW: 64 °F (18 °C)

APRIL
HIGH: 93 °F (34 °C)
LOW: 73 °F (23 °C)

JULY
HIGH: 82 °F (28 °C)
LOW: 70 °F (21 °C)

OCTOBER
HIGH: 88 °F (31 °C)
LOW: 68 °F (20 °C)

°F = degrees Fahrenheit
°C = degrees Celsius

Nigeria is a **tropical** country with rainy and dry seasons. The south experiences constant temperatures year-round and rainfall from March to November. The north is drier, with temperatures that may vary widely.

Long ago, Nigeria was home to many animals. However, many are now **endangered**. Lions and giraffes only roam the plains in protected **reserves**. In Nigeria's national parks, chimpanzees swing from tree to tree. In the low southeastern mountains, rare Cross River gorillas live quietly away from humans.

Some animals are common in Nigeria. Red river hogs trample through **rain forests**. Quail and guinea fowl run across the plains. Eagles, the national animal, soar above them. Crocodiles and hippos swim in the rivers alongside many kinds of fish.

CHIMPANZEE

RED RIVER HOGS

HARLEQUIN QUAIL

CROSS RIVER GORILLA

AFRICAN CRESTED PORCUPINE

AFRICAN
FISH EAGLE

AFRICAN FISH EAGLE

Life Span: up to 24 years
Red List Status: least concern

African fish eagle range =

LEAST CONCERN	NEAR THREATENED	VULNERABLE	ENDANGERED	CRITICALLY ENDANGERED	EXTINCT IN THE WILD	EXTINCT

▲

HOME SWEET HOME

By the year 2050, Nigeria's population is expected to pass the population of the United States. Nigeria will become the third-most populous country in the world!

Nigeria is home to over 214 million people. It has the largest population of any African country. Nigerians belong to more than 250 different **ethnic** groups. The three largest are the Hausa, the Yoruba, and the Igbo.

Just over half of the Nigerian population is Muslim. Most other Nigerians are Roman Catholic or Christian. While English is the official language of Nigeria, over 500 languages are spoken in the country. Other major languages include Yoruba, Hausa, Igbo, and Fulani.

FAMOUS FACE

Name: Chimamanda Ngozi Adichie
Birthday: September 15, 1977
Hometown: Enugu, Nigeria
Famous for: Award-winning author of novels, essays, and short stories as well as a celebrated public speaker

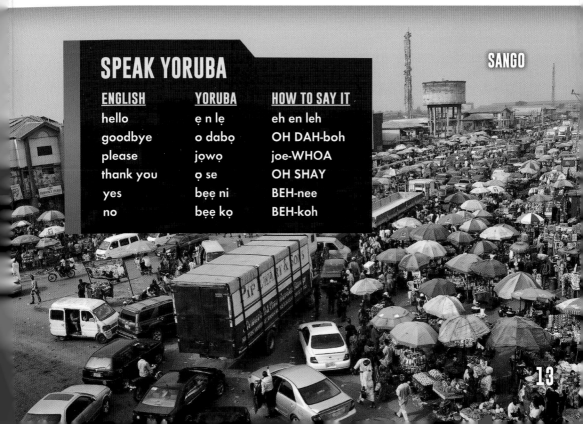

SPEAK YORUBA

ENGLISH	YORUBA	HOW TO SAY IT
hello	ẹ n lẹ	eh en leh
goodbye	o dabọ	OH DAH-boh
please	jọwọ	joe-WHOA
thank you	ọ se	OH SHAY
yes	bẹẹ ni	BEH-nee
no	bẹẹ kọ	BEH-koh

SANGO

COMMUNITIES

Half of all Nigerians live in **rural** areas. They typically live in villages ruled by a chief. Villagers are usually related by a common **ancestor**. Families live together in **compounds**. **Urban** Nigerians live in houses or apartments built of concrete or clay. In major cities such as Lagos, residents travel by bus or taxi. Trains help Nigerians travel all across the country.

AN ELECTRICAL PROBLEM

Around 100 million Nigerians live in areas without electricity. Many programs are working to bring reliable electricity to Nigerians through solutions like solar power.

LAGOS

Family is important to all Nigerians. Nigerian families are often large. They gather often to celebrate births, weddings, and holidays.

Customs vary widely by ethnic group in Nigeria, but Nigerians tend to be social people. They enjoy feasting together. When guests visit, they are always served first at a meal. Nigerians will not use the left hand when eating. They consider this hand to be unclean.

Storytelling is at the heart of Nigerian **culture**. For Nigerians, it is a form of education and entertainment. Adults tell children stories to teach them values and cultural history. Adults also enjoy stories told through theater productions with music and dance. Nigerians hope to preserve their storytelling **tradition** for many generations to come.

EDUCATION FOR ALL

Nigeria's education system struggles to keep up with its population growth. In 2017, more than ten million children did not attend school. The government has since built thousands of new schools to address this problem.

Primary education is free and required in Nigeria. It begins at age 6 and lasts for six years. In the first three years, children study in their **native** languages. Students then attend secondary schools for six years. Only three years are required. Students may choose job training instead of the last three years of high school.

Seven out of ten Nigerians work in agriculture. They may work on farms growing corn or yams. Others work on cocoa, palm oil, or rubber **plantations**. Nigerians with **manufacturing** jobs may work at paper or steel mills. Many people work in the country's coal and oil industries.

OIL WORKERS

FARMERS

SOCCER

Soccer is a favorite sport in Nigeria. The national men's soccer team, named the Super Eagles, has played in several World Cups and Olympic Games. Nigerians have also won many Olympic medals in track and field. Tennis, boxing, and wrestling are other popular sports. Nigerians also love swimming. They swim at the beach, in rivers, and at public pools across the country.

TRACK AND FIELD

Nigerians love to play board games like Scrabble and Monopoly. They also play traditional Nigerian board games like *ayo*, a game in which players move seeds around a board.

AYO

LET'S PLAY AYO!

Ayo is one of the most popular Nigerian board games. It is even played at weddings! With a friend, try making your very own ayo board game to play!

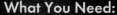

What You Need:
- an empty dozen-size egg carton
- two jars or medium-sized plastic containers
- 48 small seeds, beads, beans, pebbles, or marbles

Instructions:
1. Each player sits on one side of the board. The six cups on each side belong to the player on that side. Each player should take one jar or container to use as a "bank."
2. Place four seeds (or other chosen small object) in each of the 12 cups.
3. Choose one player to start. The starting player chooses any cup from their side of the board and takes all the seeds in it.
4. The player then puts one seed in each cup on the board, moving in a counter-clockwise direction. They skip both banks. If the last seed ends up in one of the opponent's cups with three or fewer seeds, the player may take all the seeds out of the cup and put them in their bank.
5. The opponent then takes their turn and repeats the same process.
6. The game continues until all the seeds have been collected into the banks. The player with the most seeds in their bank wins the game!

CASSAVA

Food is a celebrated part of Nigerian culture. Yams and **cassava** are common at most meals. For breakfast, *dodo*, or fried plantains, are eaten with fried eggs. Pancakes are enjoyed with coffee or tea.

Lunch and dinner dishes may include meat or seafood. Hearty soups such as *banga* are a southern specialty. Banga contains meat, fish, palm fruit, and spices. Skewers of spicy meat called *suya* are enjoyed in the northern region. *Jollof*, the national dish, features rice mixed with tomato, pepper, and onion. Puff puffs make a tasty dessert or snack.

DODO

BANGA

JOLLOF

PUFF PUFFS

Ask an adult to help you make your own puff puffs!

Ingredients:
3 cups flour
2 1/4 teaspoons quick rise yeast
1 cup sugar
1/2 teaspoon nutmeg
2 cups warm water
vegetable oil for frying

Steps:
1. Combine the dry ingredients in a mixing bowl. Slowly stir in water. Mix until the batter is smooth.
2. Cover the bowl with a towel. Let it sit for one hour at room temperature.
3. Fill a large saucepan about halfway with vegetable oil and heat over medium heat.
4. Use a spoon to scoop up the batter. Carefully drop balls of batter into the hot oil one at a time.
5. Fry the balls, flipping them until they are golden all over.
6. Remove the puff puffs from the pan with a slotted spoon. Place the puff puffs on a paper towel-covered plate. Allow to cool.

CELEBRATIONS

Nigerians celebrate Christian or Muslim holidays, depending on their faith. Christians celebrate Christmas with feasts, fireworks, and new clothes. Muslims celebrate the month of Ramadan each year. During this month, people pray and **fast**. They eat only after the sun has set.

LET'S PARTY!

The annual Durbar Festival follows Ramadan in northern Nigeria. After morning prayers, Nigerians attend a colorful celebration in the town square. Elegantly dressed horsemen salute the town leader. Then they race through the streets!

DURBAR FESTIVAL

CALABAR
CARNIVAL

On October 1, Nigerians celebrate Independence Day.
It marks the day Nigeria gained independence from Britain.
Nigerians celebrate with traditional music, parades, and feasts.
The Calabar Carnival takes place during the whole month
of December. It celebrates the **diversity** of Nigeria through
traditional dance, fashion shows, and concerts. Nigerians are
very proud of their culture!

1804
Fulani leader Usman dan Fodio begins a war to convert Nigerians to Islam and eventually brings most of northern Nigeria under his control

1000s
Nigerian kingdoms and empires are formed, including the Hausa, Oyo, and Benin kingdoms

1914
Nigeria becomes a colony of Britain, joining the northern and southern regions

LATE 1400s
Various European nations begin enslaving Nigerians and sending them to Europe and the Americas

1807
British Empire bans the slave trade and begins exporting palm oil and timber from Nigeria

1976
Lieutenant General Olusegun Obasanjo introduces a presidential constitution

2014
More than 200 girls are taken from a school by a terrorist organization

2000
Northern states adopt Islamic laws, leading to ongoing violence between Nigerian Muslims and Christians

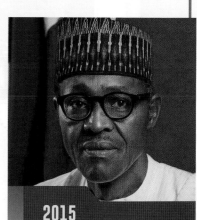

1960
Nigeria wins independence from Britain

2015
Muhammadu Buhari is elected president

NIGERIA FACTS

Official Name: Federal Republic of Nigeria

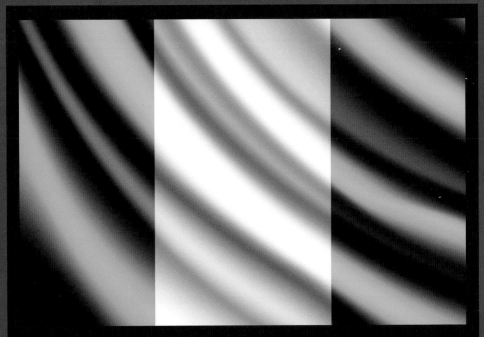

Flag of Nigeria: The Nigerian flag bears two green vertical bands with a white band in the middle. The green bands represent the forests and resources of the country. The white band stands for peace and unity.

Area: 356,669 square miles
(923,768 square kilometers)

Capital City: Abuja

Important Cities: Lagos, Kano, Ibadan

Population:
214,028,302 (July 2020)

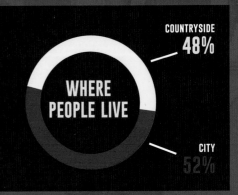

WHERE PEOPLE LIVE

COUNTRYSIDE
48%

CITY
52%

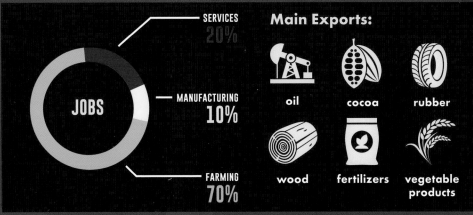

SERVICES
20%

JOBS

MANUFACTURING
10%

FARMING
70%

Main Exports:

oil

cocoa

rubber

wood

fertilizers

vegetable
products

National Holiday:
Independence Day (October 1)

Main Languages:
English (official), Yoruba, Hausa, Igbo

Form of Government:
federal presidential republic

Title for Country Leader:
president

RELIGION

MUSLIM
53.5%

OTHER
0.6%

ROMAN
CATHOLIC
10.6%

OTHER
CHRISTIAN
35.3%

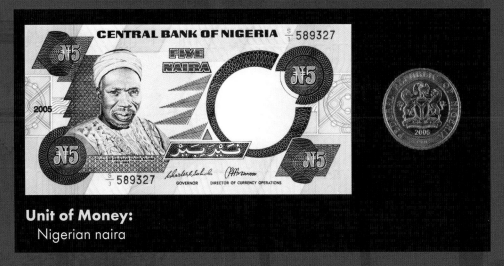

Unit of Money:
Nigerian naira

GLOSSARY

ancestor—a relative who lived long ago

cassava—a tropical plant with starchy, edible roots

compounds—enclosed areas that include groups of buildings

culture—the beliefs, arts, and ways of life in a place or society

diversity—the state of being made up of people or things that are different from one another

endangered—at risk of becoming extinct

ethnic—related to a group of people who share customs and an identity

fast—to stop eating all foods or particular foods for a time

gulf—part of an ocean or sea that extends into land

manufacturing—a field of work in which people use machines to make products

native—originally from the area or related to a group of people that began in the area

plains—large areas of flat land

plantations—large farms that grow coffee beans, cotton, rubber, or other crops; plantations are mainly found in warm climates.

plateau—an area of flat, raised land

rain forests—thick, green forests that receive a lot of rain

reserves—areas of land that are protected

rural—related to the countryside

souvenirs—items that are kept as reminders of a place

tradition—a custom, idea, or belief that is handed down from one generation to the next

tropical—part of the tropics; the tropics is a hot, rainy region near the equator.

urban—related to cities and city life

TO LEARN MORE

AT THE LIBRARY

Lynch, Annabelle. *Living in Nigeria*. London, U.K.: Franklin Watts, 2017.

Nanz, Rosie. *Explore Nigeria: 12 Key Facts.* Mankato, Minn.: 12 Story Library, 2019.

Onyefulu, Ifeoma. *The Girl Who Married a Ghost and Other Tales From Nigeria*. London, U.K.: Frances Lincoln Children's Books, 2010.

ON THE WEB

FACTSURFER

Factsurfer.com gives you a safe, fun way to find more information.

1. Go to www.factsurfer.com.

2. Enter "Nigeria" into the search box and click Q.

3. Select your book cover to see a list of related content.

INDEX

The images in this book are reproduced through the courtesy of: Lingbeek/ Getty Images, front cover; Akintunde Akinleye/ Newscom, pp. 4-5; Amaka Chidioka, p. 5 (Idanre Hill); Amaifenhenry1/ Wikipedia, p. 5 (Ogbunike Caves); Gary Cook/ Alamy, p. 5 (Yankari National Park); Tayvay, p. 5 (Zuma Rock); Pather Media GmbH/ Alamy, p. 8; Christopher Scott/ Alamy, p. 9 (top); Red Confidential, p. 9 (bottom); Eric Isselee, p. 10 (chimpanzee); RudiErnst, p. 10 (Red River hogs); Jo-anne Hounsom, p. 10 (harlequin quail); Kit Korzun, p. 10 (Cross River gorilla); Steve Bramall, p. 10 (African crested porcupine); Wang LinQiang, p. 11; agafapaperiapunta, p. 12; lev radin, p. 13 (top); Agbegiyi Adekunle Sunday, pp. 13 (bottom), 20; Irene Becker Photography/ Getty Images, p. 14; Ogunpitan Adeyemi, p. 15; i_am_zews, p. 16; Abraham Ovie Dixon, p. 17; Friedrich Stark/ Alamy, p. 18; Eye Ubiquitous/ Alamy, p. 19 (top); Thomas Imo/ Contributor/ Getty Images, p. 19 (bottom); AGIF, p. 20 (top); Aspen Photo, p. 20 (bottom); Fela Sanu, p. 21 (top); Ezume Images, p. 21 (bottom); jrroman, p. 23 (dodo); Osarieme Eweka, p. 23 (banga); -Ivinst-, p. 23 (jollof); Primestock Photography, p. 23 (puff puffs); Jorge Fernandez/ Alamy, p. 24; Anadolu Agency/ Contributor/ Getty Images, p. 25; DefenseImagery.mil/ Wikipedia, p. 26 (top); Bayo Omoboriowo/ Wikipedia, p. 26 (bottom); Glyn Thomas/ Alamy, p. 29 (banknote); Vitoria Holdings LLC/ Alamy, p. 29 (coin).